The Mystery in the Bottle

Val Willis

Pictures by

John Shelley

ANDRE DEUTSCH CHILDREN'S BOOKS

The illustrations are dedicated
to Shizeko and Timothy with love

First Published in 1991 by
André Deutsch Children's Books
an imprint of Scholastic Publications Limited
7–9 Pratt Street, London NW1 0AE

ISBN 0 233 98716 9

Printed in Singapore by Kim Hup Lee

When Bobby Bell's dad had a day off work, he decided to take Bobby and his mum to the seaside. Bobby was pleased because it meant a day off school. Miss Potts, his teacher, was pleased because it meant a day's rest from Bobby.

It was warm, sunny and peaceful when they arrived at the beach. Dad sat in a deckchair with the newspaper. Mum sat in a deckchair with a big fat book.

Bobby chased crabs round the rock pools, teased the sea anemones by dropping sand into their waving tentacles and

watched the shrimps fall through the holes in his fishing net. Bobby built a giant sandcastle with six turrets and a moat. He showed it to Dad, but Dad was asleep. Mum suggested he put shells on the turrets, so he did. Then there was nothing left to do.

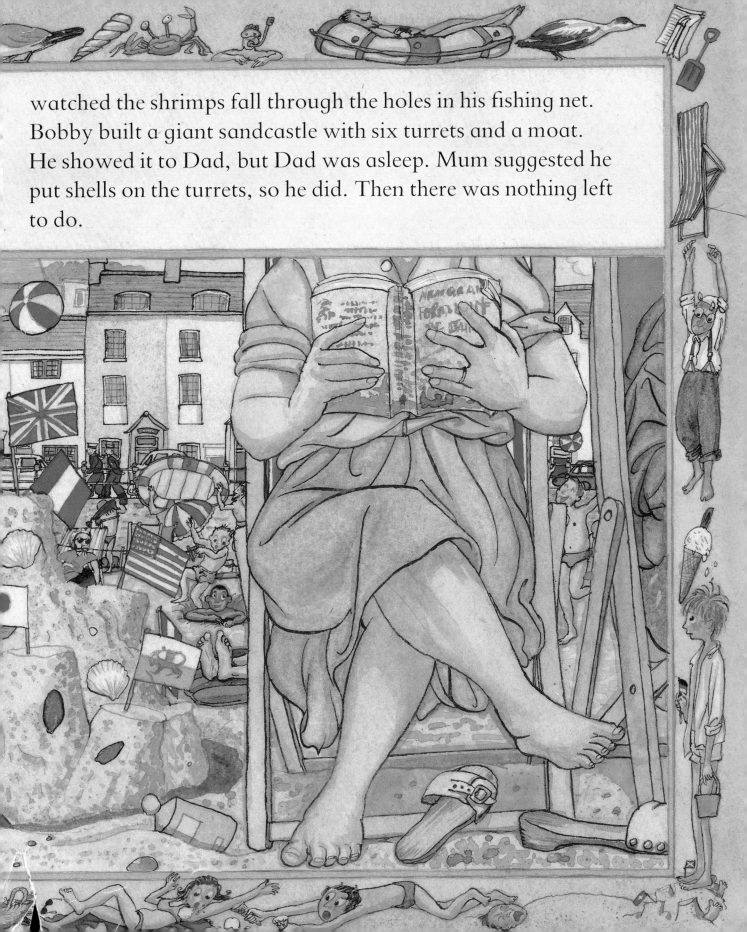

Bobby took his net and stood at the edge of the sea. He watched the waves rushing backwards and forwards over his toes, then he saw the bottle. It was bobbing on top of the foam just a little way out. Bobby scooped it up in his net.

He lifted the bottle carefully out of the net. It had a cork in the top and something strange inside it. Bobby looked closely and saw a tiny little girl with her nose pressed flat against the glass. Bobby was sure she had a fish's tail.

Bobby ran over to show his mum and dad.
"I've found a bottle," he said, "and guess what's inside it?"
"A ship," said Dad from behind his newspaper.
"A message," said Mum from behind her book.
"Wrong," said Bobby. "It's a mermaid."

"Can I take her home?" asked Bobby.
"Don't spill any water in the back of my car," said Dad.
Bobby held the bottle carefully in his hand all the way back
home. The mermaid pulled faces at him through the glass.
Bobby pulled faces back.

When they got home, Bobby ran straight upstairs and filled the basin in the bathroom with water. He uncorked the bottle and carefully poured out the little girl.

"Thanks," said the mermaid, "I was a bit squashed in that bottle and by the way I'm starving."
"I'll see what I can find in the kitchen," said Bobby.

Bobby went down for his tea and came back to see the mermaid. She seemed to fill the basin. Bobby filled the bath and carefully lifted the mermaid in.

"Thanks," she said, "I was a bit squashed in that basin.
Now what have you got me to eat?"
"Fish fingers," said Bobby.
"Fish have fins where I come from," said the mermaid.

Bobby went to school next day and left the mermaid swimming round the bath. She looked rather squashed. Bobby told Miss Potts about his day at the seaside. Miss Potts told Bobby about the school Swimming Gala.

"We have already picked the teams," she said. "Your team has Helen Wells and Sammy Price and Becky Braithwaite in it." "That's not fair," said Bobby, "two of them have only just learnt how to swim."

When Bobby got home from school, he went straight upstairs. The mermaid was lying in the bath. She seemed to fill it. Bobby told the mermaid about the Swimming Gala. "None of my team can swim very well," he said, "Helen Wells always cries, Sammy Price keeps putting his foot on the bottom and that Becky Braithwaite thinks she's the world's greatest swimmer but she's so slow."

"I love swimming galas," said the mermaid, "I'll be in your team. Anyway, I'm a bit squashed in this bath. I'd like to stretch my tail in a big pool."

"How shall I get you to school?" asked Bobby next morning.
"No problem," said the mermaid, "just bring my bottle and
I'll jump back in."

Bobby held the bottle over the side of the bath. The mermaid shrank to her original size and flipped back into the bottle. Bobby put the cork on quickly in case she changed her mind.

That afternoon, Bobby's class changed for swimming and lined up by the pool. Bobby held the bottle tightly in his hand.

"My team will win," he whispered to Peter Drew.

"I don't think so," said Peter Drew politely, "your team are hopeless."

Bobby smiled and took the cork out of the bottle. The mermaid plopped into the pool but no one seemed to notice. Mr Crump, the headmaster, shouted, "Ready, steady, go," and blew his whistle.

Bobby's team did not do well. Little Helen Wells cried.
Sammy Price kept touching the bottom and Becky
Braithwaite was SO slow.
By the time Bobby jumped in, his team was last by a long way.

Suddenly the mermaid, who had grown to her full size, flicked her tail and shot past all the others in a flurry of foam, to arrive at the end first.

"We won, we won," shouted Bobby, jumping up and down.

"Bobby Bell," yelled Miss Potts, "you're disqualified. You must have cheated."

"We'll soon see about that," said the mermaid, flicking her tail and doing a double somersault in the air.

Within seconds the pool was filled with coral and seaweed. Beautiful coloured fishes darted here and there, crabs scuttled on the bottom and an octopus inched its tentacles towards Miss Potts' chair.

All the children jumped into the pool and swam and dived with the mermaid. A dolphin appeared from nowhere and performed the most amazing tricks. The audience clapped loudly.

Mr Crump stood up and blew his whistle.
"Miss Potts," he roared, "any idea who's responsible for all this?"
"It looks like Bobby Bell again, headmaster," she said.

"Bobby Bell," roared Mr Crump over the din. "Come here."
Bobby pulled himself out of the pool and stood in front of the
headmaster.
"Bobby Bell," said Mr Crump, "sort this mess out. NOW."

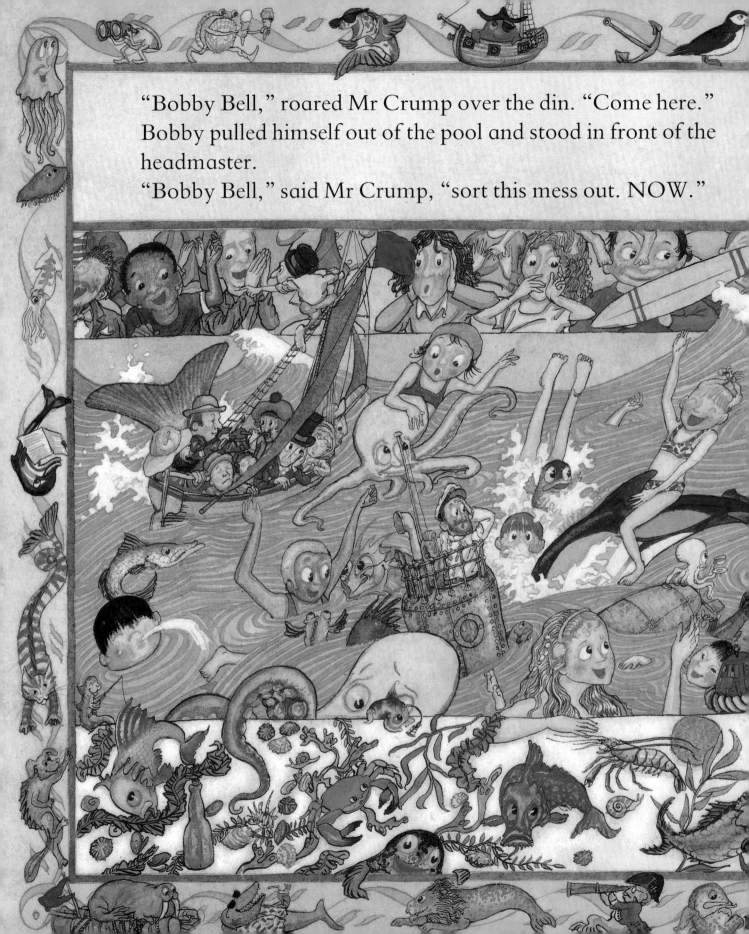

Bobby waved at the mermaid and she swam over.
"I'm in trouble again," said Bobby, "what shall I do?"
"Shame," said the mermaid, "I haven't had so much fun in years, but don't worry, I have an idea."

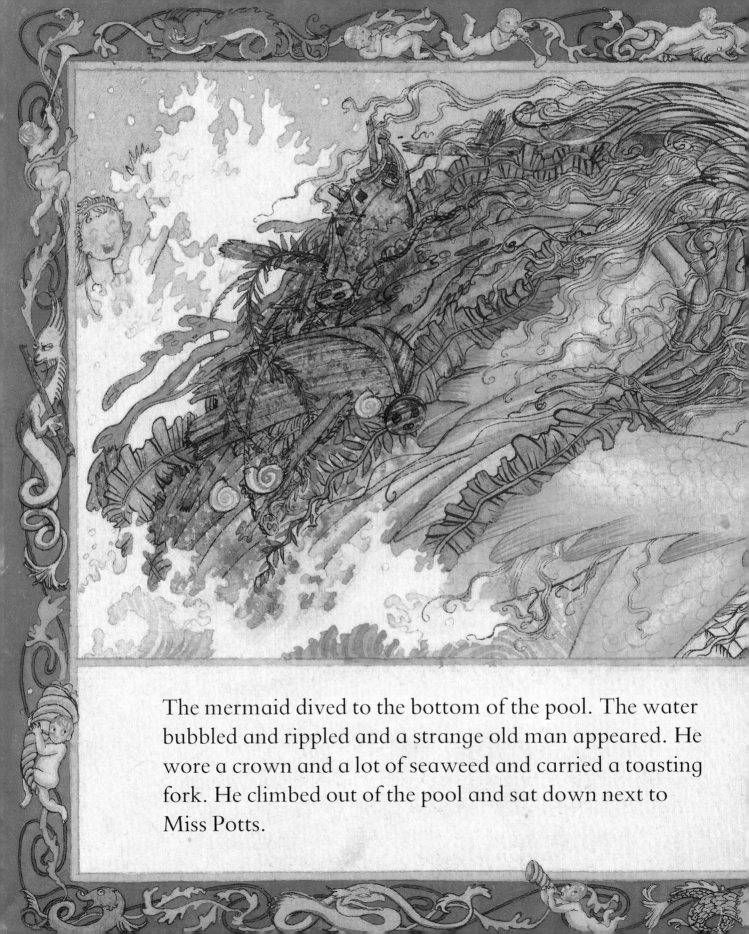

The mermaid dived to the bottom of the pool. The water bubbled and rippled and a strange old man appeared. He wore a crown and a lot of seaweed and carried a toasting fork. He climbed out of the pool and sat down next to Miss Potts.

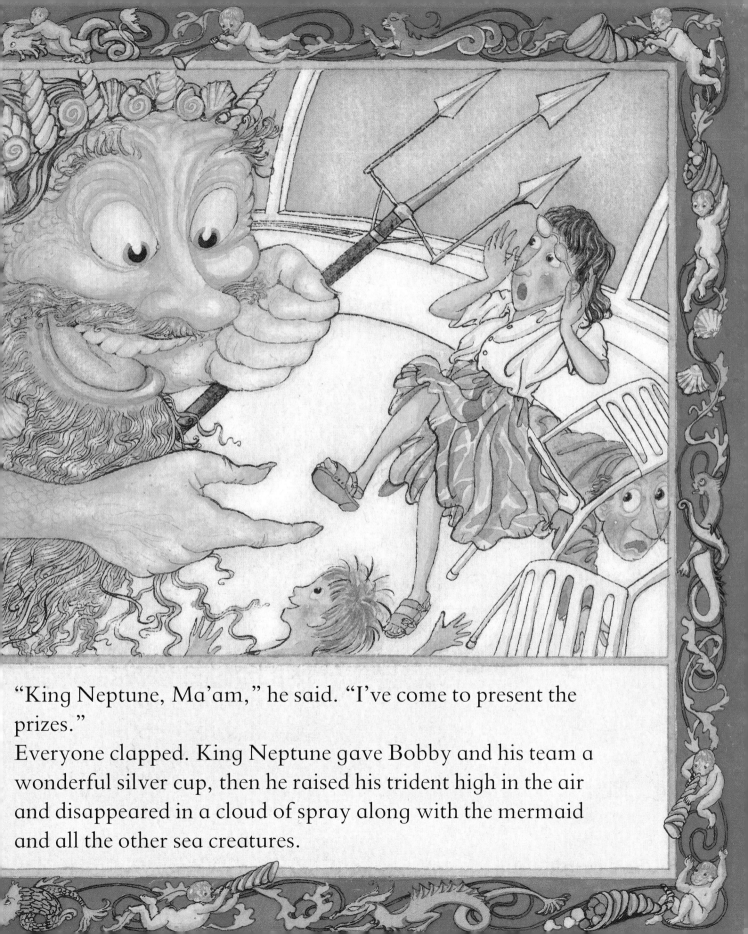

"King Neptune, Ma'am," he said. "I've come to present the prizes."

Everyone clapped. King Neptune gave Bobby and his team a wonderful silver cup, then he raised his trident high in the air and disappeared in a cloud of spray along with the mermaid and all the other sea creatures.

Bobby clutched the silver cup tightly to his chest and picked up the small glass bottle. He put the cork in the bottle and the bottle in the silver cup, then he raised the cup above his head and smiled.